For my dandelions, Star and Samantha —K.S.

For Steve Apfelbaum, who taught me about friendship and flowers, and for Stephanie and our dandelion family —R.D.

Text copyright © 2014 by Kevin Sheehan
Jacket art and interior illustrations copyright © 2014 by Rob Dunlavey

All rights reserved. Published in the United States by Schwartz & Wade Books, an imprint of Random House Children's Books, a division of Random House, Inc., New York.

Schwartz & Wade Books and the colophon are trademarks of Random House, Inc.

Visit us on the Web! randomhouse.com/kids
Educators and librarians, for a variety of teaching tools, visit us at RHTeachersLibrarians.com

Library of Congress Cataloging-in-Publication Data
Sheehan, Kevin.
The dandelion's tale / Kevin Sheehan ; [illustrations by Rob Dunlavey].—1st ed.
p. cm.
Summary: A sparrow selflessly relates Dandelion's story to the world in this tale of friendship, the power of memories, and the cycle of life.
ISBN 978-0-375-87032-3 (hc) —ISBN 978-0-375-97032-0 (glb)— ISBN 978-0-375-98890-5 (ebook)
[1. Sparrows—Fiction. 2. Dandelions—Fiction. 3. Life cycles (Biology)—Fiction.
4. Friendship—Fiction.] I. Dunlavey, Rob, ill. II. Title.
PZ7.S5393Dan 2014 [E]—dc23 2012027440

The text of this book is set in New Aster.
The illustrations were rendered in ink, watercolor,
colored pencil, crayon, and digital media.
Book design by Rachael Cole

MANUFACTURED IN CHINA
10 9 8 7 6 5 4 3 2 1
First Edition

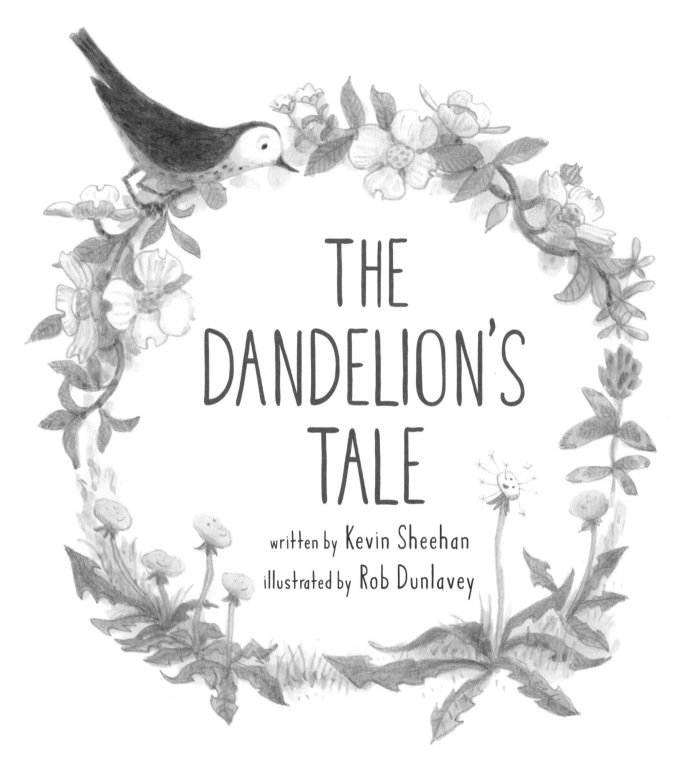

THE DANDELION'S TALE

written by Kevin Sheehan

illustrated by Rob Dunlavey

schwartz & wade books · new york

One fine summer day, Sparrow was out flying above a beautiful green meadow. The warm sun felt wonderful against his brown, spotted feathers.

Stopping to rest on the limb of a dogwood tree, Sparrow noticed
a dandelion, alone in the tall grass. Her downy seeds looked like
a delicate cotton ball perched atop her light green stem.

Imagine Sparrow's surprise when he heard the dandelion crying.

"Hello down there," Sparrow chirped. "Why the tears? The sun
is out, the air is warm and everything is in bloom."

"Let me tell you why I'm sad," the dandelion replied as Sparrow fluttered down beside her.

"A short while ago, I was so strong, and the
brightest yellow you've ever seen. Now I'm white and
fuzzy and I've lost most of my seedpods. If the wind
starts to blow, I'll lose them all and no one will
know I was ever here."

Sparrow counted the dandelion's remaining
pods—"1-2-3-4-5-6-7-8-9-10." Inside, each held
a tiny seed.

"Oh dear," Sparrow replied. "What will you do?"

The dandelion considered her dilemma.
"Since I'm planted in the ground and have
no arms or legs, maybe *you* can help me."

"That's the spirit!" Sparrow chirped. "Just tell me how."

The dandelion thought for a moment, then said, "Can you fly me over to the other dandelions so I can tell them about myself?"

Sparrow flew into the air and quickly
scanned the fields.
There wasn't another dandelion in sight.

"I don't see any others," he reported. "There are some in a field I pass every day, but I'm afraid that may be too far away. The breeze could blow your seedpods right off."

The dandelion sighed. "Still, if I could have only one wish, I would wish to be remembered."

"Wait! I have an idea!" Sparrow exclaimed, hopping from foot to foot. "I could write your story in that patch of dirt by the tree."

"It would be just like a book!" the dandelion said with glee. "I once saw a young mother read to her little boy there. The story was wonderful, and I was so envious that people have something as marvelous as books."

Sparrow flapped his wings and landed by the tree. "I know you can't see me," he shouted. "Just tell me what you want to write."

The dandelion was thrilled.
There were so many things to say.

"Write that I like the
smell of the meadow the
day after it rains.

"Oh, and that I love to
look at clouds against a
blue afternoon sky."

"Write how much I've enjoyed hearing the laughter of children as they play in the meadow,

and the fun I've had talking with the squirrels as they look for food in the morning."

Sparrow wrote and wrote for
hours, scratching the dandelion's words
into the soft, dry dirt. The dandelion told him
all the things she had seen and loved.

She spoke of milkweed and hummingbirds;
of dancing butterflies and picnicking families;
of busy ants and busier bees.

When they were done, Sparrow read everything back to the dandelion.

"It's perfect," she said. "Thank you so much. You have made me very happy."

To show his own happiness, the sparrow whistled a song. By the time he was finished, shadows were creeping across the meadow and night was falling. "I have to go now," he told the dandelion. "But I'll be back tomorrow and we can read your story again." And with a loud chirp, he spread his wings and flew home.

That night, there was a terrible storm. Thunder rumbled. Lightning lit up the sky. "Oh my!" Sparrow cried. "I do hope the dandelion is all right."

He tried to fly to the meadow, but the
wind blew him back into his nest.

Defeated, Sparrow decided that he would visit the dandelion first thing in the morning.

Morning came, and with it, the sun rose in the sky. Rustling the water from his feathers, Sparrow sprang from his nest and flew to the dogwood tree.

But all that was left of the dandelion was her light green stem. The storm had been too powerful for the fragile little flower.

"Poor, poor Dandelion.
I will miss you," he said.

Then Sparrow recalled the dandelion's tale.

"At least I still have your story to share," he said.

He hopped over to the dirt patch. But his scratches were gone. The dandelion's story had been washed away by the rain.

Sparrow closed
his eyes and wept. As the
breeze blew gently through the
trees, he said, "I promise I will never
forget you." And he began to sing a
beautiful song about the dandelion for
all in the meadow to hear. Even the
other birds in the trees joined in
the dandelion's song.

A few weeks later, Sparrow was flying over the meadow when
he saw a cluster of baby dandelions by the dogwood tree. Curious,
he set down in the middle of them. "Hello there," he said.

"Hi," they replied in their tiny voices.

Sparrow counted the flowers—"1-2-3-4-5-6-7-8-9-10"—just
as there had been ten white seedpods on the dandelion.

Each of the dandelion's children was as bright and yellow
as the sun.

"Would you like to hear a special story?" Sparrow asked.

"Yes, please," the littlest dandelion said.

Sparrow settled into the grass and cleared his throat with a slight chirp. "I'm going to tell you about a great friend of mine."

And because Sparrow had written and read the
dandelion's story, he discovered that he knew it by heart.
When he was finished, he felt sure that the dandelion
would never be forgotten.

She would always live on in the bright yellow petals of her children, and their children, and so on until the end of time.